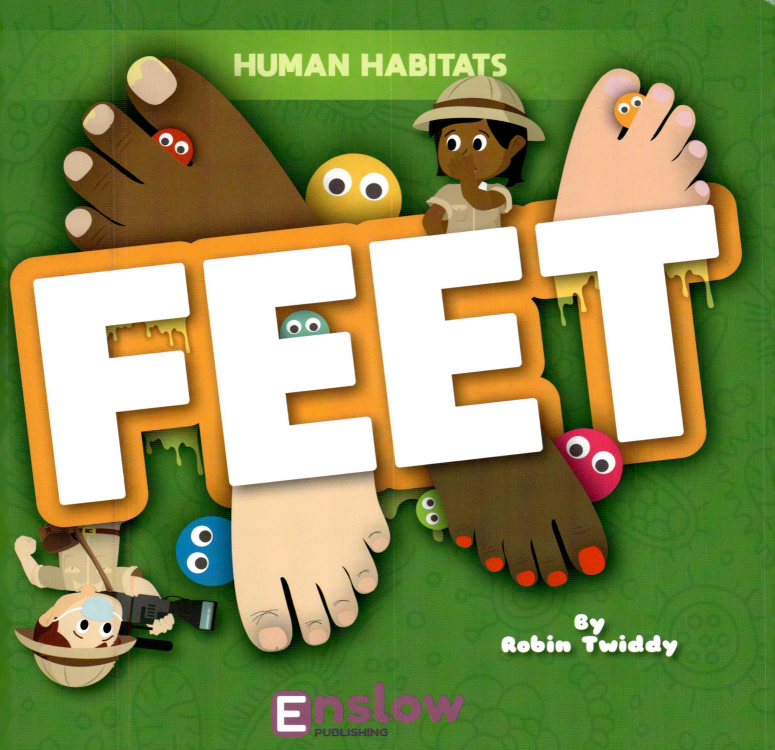

HUMAN HABITATS

FEET

By Robin Twiddy

Enslow PUBLISHING

Published in 2022 by Enslow Publishing, LLC
101 W. 23rd Street, Suite 240,
New York, NY 10011

Copyright © 2022 Booklife Publishing
This edition published by arrangement with Booklife Publishing

All rights reserved.

No part of this book may be reproduced by any means without the written permission of the publisher.

Cataloging-in-Publication Data

Names: Twiddy, Robin.
Title: Feet / Robin Twiddy.
Description: New York : Enslow Publishing, 2022. | Series: Human habitats | Includes glossary and index.
Identifiers: ISBN 9781978523524 (pbk.) | ISBN 9781978523548 (library bound) | ISBN 9781978523531 (6 pack) | ISBN 9781978523555 (ebook)
Subjects: LCSH: Foot--Juvenile literature. | Human physiology--Juvenile literature.
Classification: LCC QL950.7 T95 2022 | DDC 591.47'9--dc23

Designer: Gareth Liddington
Editor: John Wood

Printed in the United States of America

CPSIA compliance information: Batch #CS22ENS: For further information contact Enslow Publishing, New York, New York at 1-800-542-2595

TRICKY WORDS

Bacterium = singular (one bacterium)
Bacteria = plural (many bacteria)
Bacterial = to do with a bacterium or many bacteria

Fungus = singular (one fungus)
Fungi = plural (many fungi)
Fungal = to do with a fungus or many fungi

Photo credits:
Cover - Shany Muchnik, 4 - ONYXprj, 6 - Designua, VectorPlotnikoff, Vectors Bang, 10 - Thor Biliavskyi, 18 - suesse, 20 - hvostik, 22 - T VECTOR ICONS.

Images are courtesy of Shutterstock.com. With thanks to Getty Images, Thinkstock Photo, and iStockphoto.

All facts, statistics, web addresses and URLs in this book were verified as valid and accurate at time of writing. No responsibility for any changes to external websites or references can be accepted by either the author or publisher.

CONTENTS

Page 4   Welcome to the Human Habitat
Page 6   A Perfect Place for Fungi
Page 8   Fungal Defenders
Page 10   Fungi Gone Wild!
Page 12   Who Knows What's Between the Toes?
Page 14   From Heel to Toe, Where Does the Bacteria Go?
Page 16   Hard Times at Heel High
Page 18   Surprise Parasite!
Page 20   Toenail or Not Toenail
Page 22   Clip Clip, Ping, Bye!

Page 24   Glossary and Index

Words that look like <u>this</u> can be found in the glossary on page 24.

WELCOME TO THE HUMAN HABITAT

Hi! I'm Mini Ventura. My cameraman, Dave, and I have been shrunk down so we can make a nature documentary all about the tiny things living in and on us. Follow us into the human habitat – a world within a world.

Face

Lungs

Hair

Mouth

Just like planet Earth, with its different habitats and the different animals living in them, the human body has many different places that are home to lots of tiny living things. Today, we will be exploring the feet and just a few of the things living in and on them.

A PERFECT PLACE FOR FUNGI

As we travel on the rolling plains of the underfoot, we see a perfect habitat for tiny life. From the peaks of heel hill to the steamy rain forests between the toes, there is all sorts of life on the foot.

The human habitat has lots of places where <u>fungi</u> like to live, but nowhere has as many types of fungus as the feet. Feet are often damp and kept in the dark. This is the perfect habitat for fungi.

Fungi are different from animals, plants, and <u>bacteria</u>. They can be big, such as mushrooms and toadstools, or as tiny as bacteria.

Toes

Heel

FUNGAL DEFENDERS

Most fungi found on the foot are not bad fungi. They do not hurt the <u>host</u> foot – they actually protect the foot from other dangerous tiny living things.

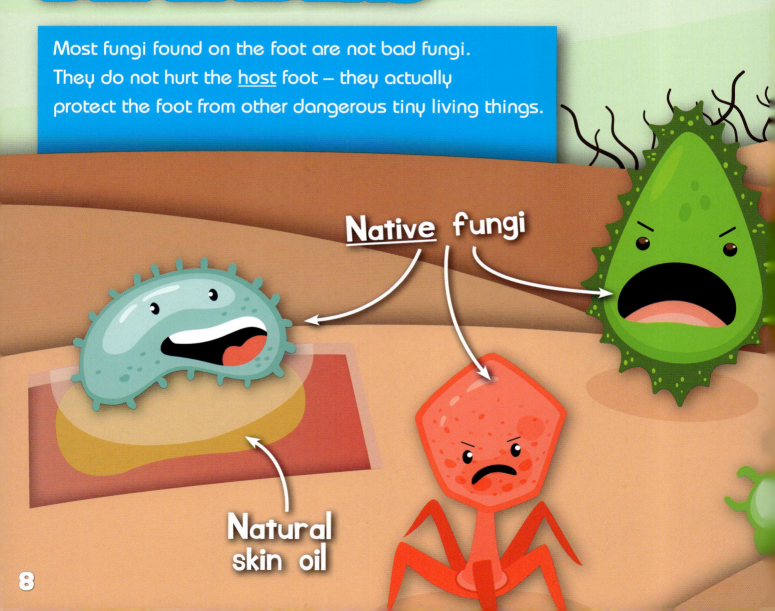

<u>Native</u> fungi

Natural skin oil

If we watch carefully, we might see something strange. The fungi on the feet eat the oils that are made by the skin. When they eat this oil, it helps protect and repair the skin. What helpful fungi!

FUNGI GONE WILD!

Those same helpful fungi can become a real problem for the human habitat. The fungi can get out of control if they have the chance to grow too big or <u>multiply</u> too much.

WHO KNOWS WHAT'S BETWEEN THE TOES?

Deep between the toes, a fungus known as athlete's foot is hard at work. This fungus loves warm and damp places.

Flaky skin

The fungus is eating away at the skin here. This will lead to flaking of the skin and even cracking. If this fungus is left to keep going, it could do some real damage to this habitat.

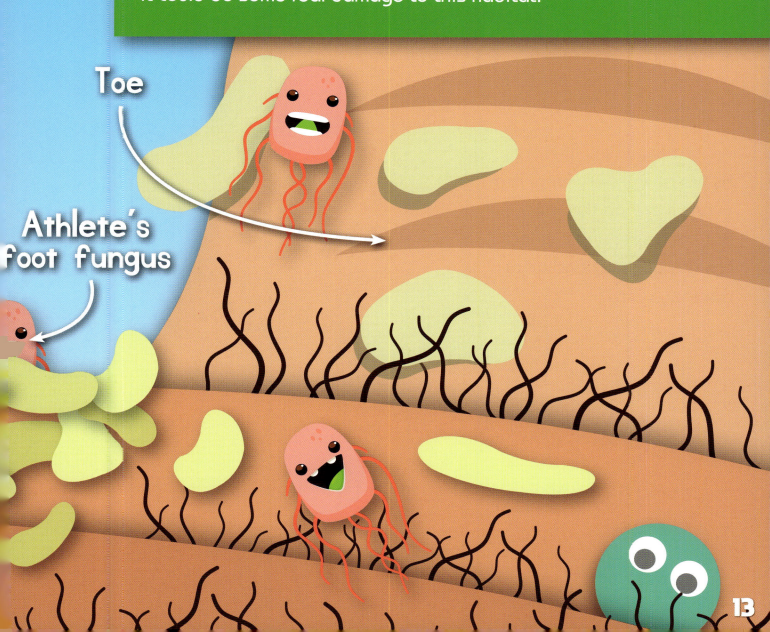

Toe

Athlete's foot fungus

FROM HEEL TO TOE, WHERE DOES THE BACTERIA GO?

As we have seen, fungi are everywhere on the feet. But the question is, where are the bacteria and what are they up to?

Flaky skin

Bacterium

HARD TIMES AT HEEL HIGH

High on the hill known as the heel, we find a large group of fungi. There are between 80 and 100 different types of fungus living on the feet, and lots of them can be found on the heel.

Dave, there are cracks all over this foot. Watch where you put your feet!

These fungi are mostly harmless unless they find a way inside the foot. If the top layers of the heel crack, then the fungi will get in and cause some real problems.

These cracks can be caused by lots of different things, but one of the main reasons is the skin getting too dry.

SURPRISE PARASITE!

Jigger burrowing

Not far from the toes and athlete's foot, a very strange sight can be seen. It would seem that there is a visitor! This creature is called a jigger flea.

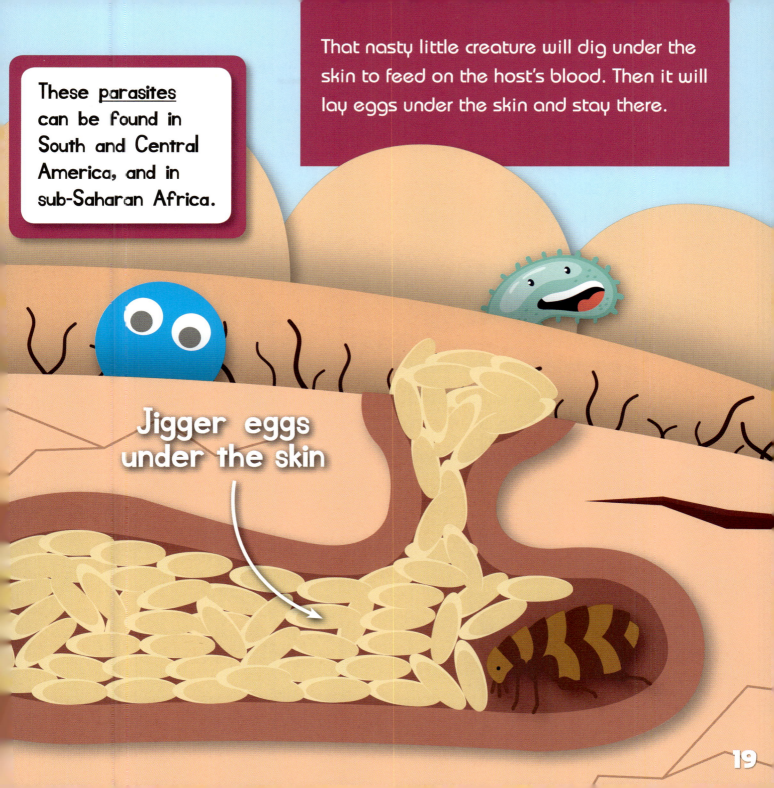

TOENAIL OR NOT TOENAIL

From here, atop the toenail, we can see the jigger at work. But while she is digging, there is activity up here on the nail.

"It is much safer here on the edge of the nail."

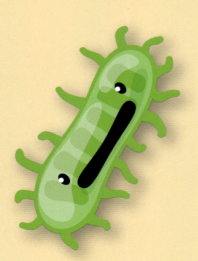

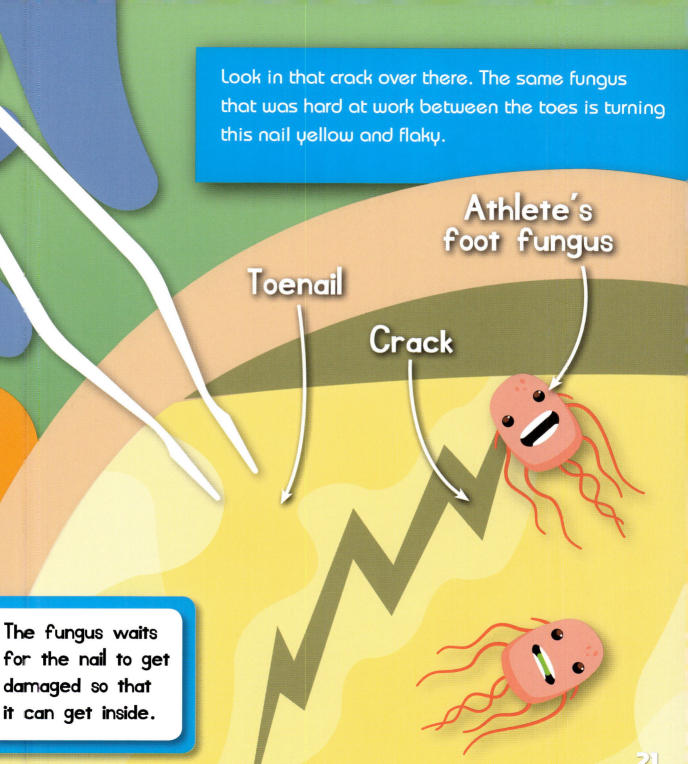

Look in that crack over there. The same fungus that was hard at work between the toes is turning this nail yellow and flaky.

Athlete's foot fungus

Toenail

Crack

The fungus waits for the nail to get damaged so that it can get inside.

CLIP CLIP, PING, BYE!

From here, at the very edge of the toenail of the big toe, we can see all the life that grows on the foot — from the fungi to the bacteria to the yucky parasites!

GLOSSARY

bacteria	tiny living things, too small to see, that can cause diseases
balanced	describing when opposite things are equal
documentary	a film that looks at real facts and events
fungi	living things that often look like plants but have no flowers
habitat	the natural home in which animals, plants, and other living things live
host	an animal or plant in or on which a parasite lives
infection	an illness caused by dirt, germs, or bacteria getting into the body
invading	entering a place which something is not from and not welcome in
multiply	to become more and more in number
native	belonging to or being from a place
parasites	creatures that live on or in another creature

INDEX

bacteria 7, 9, 14–15, 22
cracks 13, 15–17, 21
damp 7, 11–12
fleas 18
fungi 7–14, 16–17, 21–22

infections 15
oils 8–9
skin 5, 8–9, 12–15, 17, 19
smell 11
socks 11